Captive In The Dark

Copyright

First Edition, February 2025

Published by: Carxander Publishing
Wisconsin

Dedication

Everyone loves a little darkness, danger, and depravity…, right? RIGHT? To all of us out there who like a hand necklace… or two… Be a good girl, now…

Opening Quote

There's an empty hole inside my chest 'cause I didn't have a heart. Looking at my past, it's a map of all my scars. And that will awaits for me, cry me a river. When it's over, and I'm shaking, here's the reapers.

I'm asking for mercy. And you know it hurts me. It's killing me slowly not to know... Will I be unforgiven? I said the prayers, but no one listened. When my life goes up in flames, who will meet me at the Gates? With all of my addictions, will I be unforgiven? Will I be unforgiven?

Unforgiven by Ryan Jesse

Chapter One

Blair

"So, we'll pay and go back to your place? How do you want this to work?" the guy in front of me asks over his menu.

I roll my eyes behind mine. We haven't even ordered yet. I guess that's what I get for trying to find love off Tinder. It's a hookup app. Obviously, that's what everyone wants when they use Tinder. A hookup. Completely my mistake in thinking there could be a decent human on the damn thing.

I clear my throat. "One step at a time, don't you think?" I lower the menu and give my date a sweet smile. "See where it all goes."

I can see the literal moment when the guy's facade slips. He quickly masks his disappointment and throws a cocky grin at me. "Sure. Of course."

Oh boy.

I go back to perusing my menu. I expect I'll be paying for my own meal tonight, so I look for something in my budget. I'd never expect anyone to pay for me, so I always make sure I can order something I can pay for on my own. Going over my budget might mean I'm going out of theirs, too. I'm always cautious of that. This restaurant is extremely classy. I didn't want to come here, but I guess this guy can't be seen slumming it anywhere else on a first date. At least that's what his rented Ferrari tells me.

I chuckle a little to myself. My lips twitch, but it's the only sign I give that I'm amused. He doesn't even realize the rental tag is in plain view. I didn't say anything because he really must feel the need to impress me. He even went all out with the designer suit. Who knows if it's a rental. Maybe it's the only suit he owns. Who am I to judge?

"I'm definitely going with the Surf 'N' Turf," he says.

I set my menu down and nod. "That looks good. Their steak is phenomenal here. I've had it once a while ago. I'm going for that and a baked potato."

The guy sets his menu down. Jeff. That's his name. I forgot it for a while. "The steak is delicious, but do you think you should be going for that?"

I raise an eyebrow. "Excuse me?"

"Well, I just think a woman of you're…" He trails off and looks me up and down. I narrow my eyes and lean forward slightly, resting my forearms on the edge of the table, daring him to continue. "...body type should be eating more salads over red meats."

I raise an eyebrow. I did not get dolled up in perfect makeup, perfect hair, and a perfect, little black dress for someone to tell me to eat salad. I'm already a small woman. I'm just over five feet. I hardly weigh more than a hundred pounds soaking wet. The heaviest parts of me are my long hair and size C tits. I already have a weight complex I'm just starting to get over. I will not allow this to set me back.

Even though I can feel it already starting.

Dammit.

Before I can say anything, the server comes to our table, and I quickly shut my mouth as he smiles down at me. "Ready to order, miss?"

I give him my first genuine smile of the night. "Yes. I'll take -"

"She'll take the steak salad. No dressing. Hold the onions and croutons. Water to drink," Jeff interrupts. I'm so dumbfounded, it's turned me speechless.

The server gives me an apologetic look as he nods and turns his head to Jeff. "And for you, sir?"

"I'll take the Surf 'N' Turf. Rare. Smother it in onions and mushrooms. And give me some extra butter for that lobster. I'll take an extra roll, too. And grab me another beer."

The server gives him a nod of disgust that almost makes me laugh. "Yes, sir."

"Actually," I interrupt. "Can you please just cancel my order? I won't be staying." I slip him a twenty as I stand. I don't say another word. I turn on my perfect, red Stilettos and leave the restaurant. I don't need to look behind me to know that Jeff's mouth is hanging open as he watches me leave.

When I get outside, I take a deep, steadying breath of the cool air. Spark, Nevada, is such a beautiful place. The air is so clean. People are nice. Well, unless they have a dick between their legs. Maybe there's a few nice ones out there, but I've managed to date all bad ones. Kinda crazy for a woman who's only twenty-two and just graduated from college.

I look down at my phone and start ordering myself a Lyft, but I'm quickly distracted by the rumbling of a powerful sounding engine. I look up as one of the sleekest looking Supersport Motorcycles I've ever seen gets closer and closer to the curb I'm near. The biker, who looks to be just as muscular and powerful as the sexy bike between his thighs, stops at a red light.

I inhale a sharp breath when he looks at me. The mirrored visor of his black helmet is down. All I can see is myself, but I feel his eyes burning into my soul. He's wearing jeans and a long sleeve, black shirt. He looks incredibly muscular.

And tall.

Sleek and sexy as the bike he rides.

With one gloved hand, he flips up his visor and shoots me a wink that has my panties burning right off my body. His eyes are a piercing blue with the most beautiful flecks of silver that accents their beauty.

"What the fuck, bitch?" Jeff says as he grabs my arm.

I try to wrench it away, but I don't get far. "Let go!" I command as loudly and forcefully as possible so everyone around me knows I don't want this.

"No one embarasses me like that! Get back in there and quit your hissy fit," Jeff growls. His profile said he was six feet, but he's not. I'd say more like five-eight, but he's got gym muscles I'm struggling with. He's stronger than me.

I pull away as hard as I can. "Let go! I'm not going back in there with you!"

"Stop acting like a spoiled brat and finish the date! Then I'll never contact you again."

"Leave me alone, Jeff!" I try to push him as I pull away, but he only grabs my other arm. I try to push off him again, but it's no use.

"Stop embarrassing yourself." He tries to drag me back into the restaurant, but I fight hard.

Finally, he loses his grip just enough that I fly backwards. I expect to fall flat on my ass and ruin my pretty dress, but that's not what happens.

Instead, I hit a solid chest. Strong arms wrap around my waist, keeping me steady. A strong, masculine scent envelopes me. I don't know what it is, but it's an unforgettable smell, especially mixed with the natural scent of the one wearing it. I feel safer than I've ever felt before, but it also makes my mouth water.

"Who the fuck are you? This isn't your concern," Jeff says, attempting to sound tough. It doesn't work. I can hear the quake of fear in his voice.

The man steadies me, and I realize all at once when I see the bike parked at the curb that the person steading me is the biker. He's taller than I thought, and a whole hell of a lot more muscular. My breath catches in my throat, but I manage to let it out when the biker focuses his attention on Jeff.

"She said let her go," he rumbles. His voice comes from somewhere low in his chest. It's deep and intimidating, but I can hear the sex oozing from every syllable. Jeff tries grabbing for me again, but this time, the biker simply moves himself in front of me. "She said… let… her… go… Walk away, little man."

"Dude, fuck you. You can have that fat bitch." Jeff spins on his heel and walks away.

I put my arms around my middle and close my eyes. I have to steady my breathing. If I don't, intrusive thoughts will get me. The thoughts that always make me feel like I'm fat. Like I need to weigh less. Eat less. Look even skinnier than I do. It's taken me years to get to the point I am now. To a point where I feel and look healthy.

"Hey, don't listen to him. He's an asshole," the biker says. I don't answer. I focus on my breathing, trusting this complete stranger to protect me and let me get myself right.

Finally, I let out a slow breath and open my eyes as I shiver. "I didn't expect it to get chilly tonight," I say, changing the subject.

The biker nods and looks up at the clear, night sky. "Yeah. It is a little bit." He looks down at me. He still hasn't taken his helmet off, and I don't know why that's so sexy. "You need a ride outta here?"

"Oh… um…" Every part of me wants to say yes, but I'm a smart woman. Going home on the back of this bike makes me too vulnerable. "I can call a Lyft." Because that's so much safer. Getting in the back of a stranger's car.

The biker chuckles like he can read my mind. "Sure."

I quickly use my app for a Lyft while the biker leans against his bike. I can feel his eyes on me as he crosses his arms across his chest and his feet at the ankles.

I force a nervous smile as I look up. "All done. Should be here shortly. They were only around the block."

"Okay." The biker takes his phone out of his pocket and starts scrolling through it nonchalantly.

I'm not sure how to take being dismissed by the guy who just saved me, but I also know the guy owes me absolutely nothing. I don't really have much time to think about it because my Lyft shows up.

I clear my throat and extend my hand. "Thank you. For your help."

Not taking his eyes off his phone or hand out of his glove, the biker shakes my hand. My heart skips a beat, and an electric jolt shoots up my arm. When he drops my hand, I feel like I might faint.

I don't. Instead, I hurry to the car and jump in the backseat. I close my eyes and finally allow myself to breathe.

"What a night," I say quietly, mostly to myself. The woman driving gives me a warm smile and strikes up a conversation.

I listen and talk to her, grateful my driver is a female, but my mind is solely on the biker. I don't allow myself to look back, but I know he's following.

Not only can I hear him…

…I feel him…

Chapter Two

Zade

I follow the Black Sedan to a duplex in a part of town I question the safety of. It looks nice enough, but I have a buddy who lives around here. He said the area is owned by a gang. He should know. He's the leader of it. Wouldn't guess it from looking at the place or him, but there are signs everywhere when a person is paying attention.

Like the tennis shoes strung up over some wires in front of a house a couple doors down from my new obsession's place. Most might not see it as anything more than some kids seeing if they could get the shoes up there, but I know better. I see right away the house is a drug house. It looks kept up, but I'd bet my life that lights are always on, and people are always coming and going at all hours of the night. The shoes are a subtle symbol. A beacon to buyers.

And to those who know what it all means, it's a very real sign to stay the fuck away from the goings on. Quiet neighborhoods are the best place for that shit to go down. No one suspects a thing unless they pay attention. Which they don't.

My buddy is a good guy, for the most part. Business man. Works downtown in one of those big skyscrapers. At night, though, things are different. He's a dangerous man, just as I am. It's probably why we get along so well. We grew up the same. Became hard and cold just the same. We're both into some dark shit. The difference is he keeps my hands clean, even though they're dirty as hell if anyone looks too closely.

I watch the girl I met downtown step carefully out of the Sedan before she leans back in. After a few moments, she stands straight once more and directs her gaze to me. I'm probably scaring the shit out of her, but I'm not going anywhere until she's safely inside her house with the doors locked. She doesn't know it, but I'm not the only one who followed her. The only difference between me and the jackass from the restaurant giving her a hard time is I'm not the one who got run off the road.

Not to say the fucker didn't try.

Too bad for him, really. That Ferrari he was driving looked like a sweet ride. Might have to buy myself one. I could afford it without an issue. I'm one of the biggest biker influencers on social media, but that's not where I make the majority of my money. It's from the merch I sell. I'm not just online. I'm partnered with major companies. My products are in every store from Walmart to Target all the way up to Cycle Gear and RevZilla. I sell everything from hoodies to actual gear a biker needs to be safe.

The girl smiles softly at me, and my jeans are instantly tighter. Painfully. Good thing I'm stopped because I need to adjust myself. There are advantages to being well-endowed, but there are also disadvantages. One of them is having to adjust a hard cock so it's not all bunched up at the seam of my jeans, and then managing to get it to lay so it's out of the way. Not easy with a ten-incher.

I'm far enough away so my dream girl can't see what I'm doing, but she has to make it harder for me when she starts walking towards me.

Fuck.

I could take off. It wouldn't be hard to gun my Kawasaki Ninja ZX-10R Supersport. The engine is a thousand cc's. I'd be gone before she has a chance to take another step.

That's what I should do.

It's not what I do.

What I actually do is move forward so I'm near her. What I actually do is melt at her smile. Damn thing is my kryptonite. No. Her sweet voice is. It's melodic. Soothes my dark soul. Fills in the empty place my heart should be.

Who am I fucking kidding? It's her. She's my kryptonite, and I have no reason for it. I come from a dark place. A very dark background. I was raised by a man so heartless that I'm sure it will be felt for generations. My mom left me with the monster when I was barely out of her womb. She didn't want kids. Neither did he. I've always wondered why he didn't throw me away. It would've been more merciful than what he put me through.

It's because of him I've never fallen in love. I've never allowed myself to. I've been on this planet for thirty-four years. I put myself through school and made my own way. I've had girls in my bed, but no one has ever stayed. I've never let them. No woman has ever had this effect on me. Certainly not one I don't even know.

But this one. There's something damn special about this one. Something I can sense and definitely don't want to let go. I need more of her. All of her.

Even her scent, soft and pure fucking female, makes me want more. I'm drooling for her. My entire being wants to consume her. Possess her.

I look her up and down before I lift my visor. She stops at my handlebars and gently caresses the grip. I choke down a groan. I'd give anything for her to touch my cock like that.

"I should really give up the dating scene. I'm apparently really bad at it and need random strangers to save me."

She can't see it, but she gets me to give her a crooked smile. "Probably."

"Fuck Tinder, right?"

I raise an eyebrow, but my heart quickens. "Tinder? What the hell's a girl like you doing on an app like that?"

She shrugs. Her eyes stay glued to my bike. "Getting in trouble, obviously." I watch her shoulders rise as she takes a deep breath. "You're right, though. A girl like me shouldn't be on an app like that." She glances at her door and bites her lip. Why does she sound broken?

"You really shouldn't be on any of those apps. Not a girl like you."

She chuckles a little as she nods. "Yeah…" She stops touching my bike, and I have to fight myself from reaching for her hand and putting it back. My imagination was running wild thinking about her touching me the way she was my bike. "Thanks for stopping. And for… well, making sure I got home, I guess."

"Sure thing, little mouse."

She still doesn't look up at me, and I'm dying for her to. Her electric golden eyes are enough to make a man drown and pretend she's his, even if it's just for a few seconds. I'd kill to see them for just a moment. Just as I'd kill to run my hands through that silky, dark hair of hers.

I see her smile shyly as she pushes some hair behind her ear, but when I still can't get her to look at me, I reach for her hand. I still have my riding gloves on, but I can feel the same spark I felt earlier when I touched her. It's like this girl has ignited me into a whole forest fire.

"Doesn't look like you can carry pepper spray in that little purse," I say. My voice is dangerously close to giving my lust for her away. Thankfully, it doesn't.

To my complete joy, she looks up at me briefly, and I catch a glimpse of those eyes. The eyes I'll be dreaming of tonight. "Oh, it just has some money, a credit card, and my ID in it."

I don't let go of her hand. I can't. "You really should carry pepper spray around. In case you need it for asshole's like that." I rub her hand with my thumb before she gently pulls it away. I let her because I don't want to freak her out. I'm already doing a good job of freaking myself out.

Fuck. This girl is everything I've ever dreamed and more.

"Don't I need a permit for that?"

"No. You just have to be eighteen and be using it to protect yourself. You're at least eighteen, right?"

She nods and pushes more of her hair behind her ear. "Yeah."

Damn. I hoped she'd tell me her age, at least. "Pepper spray. Good option. If you're gonna be using dating apps and hookup apps, best to be safe."

She nods and looks towards her house. "I should go. It's pretty cold out here…" She smiles when she looks back at me. "Thank you again."

And like that, she's out of my grasp. She hurries to her door and lets herself in. I notice that a porch light doesn't come on. She doesn't seem to have any motion activated lights at all. Which likely means she doesn't have cameras. Probably not even an alarm. No safety features at all.

When she closes her door, I wait until I see a light come on. Once it does, I see her stand near the window. She gives me a little wave. I don't want to leave, but I do. I gun my engine and pop a wheelie just for her on my way down the street. Once I hit the stop sign at the end of her block, I drop my front wheel on the pavement and take off once more. I don't stop at the sign. I already checked and saw there was no one coming.

On my way home, the girl doesn't leave my thoughts. I make it my mission to get her that pepper spray because I don't think she'll buy it herself. She doesn't seem like the type who spends much money on herself or her safety, so if she doesn't, I damn well will.

Chapter Three

Blair

I run my finger around the can of pepper spray in the pink carrying case that I found on my doorstep this morning. I looked around, hoping to catch a glimpse of the sexy biker who filled my dreams, but there was no sign of him. I went to work disappointed, worked my whole shift, and then finally just got home.

My mind has been on the biker the entire time. I even got in trouble at work because I kept getting distracted. As I sit on my front porch waiting for my Lyft, I've never wanted a camera system more. Maybe I could've caught a glimpse of him when he put the pepper spray by my door. Maybe that would've soothed this ache that I have for him.

The sexy stranger with the sexy voice on the sexy bike.

My Lyft finally shows. I have my own car, but I don't drive it to dates. I feel like it's safer that way. Nothing to track them to me if they turn out to be creeps, which I seem to attract like bees to honey.

I hurry to my Lyft and climb in the backseat. Per the biker, I'm carrying pepper spray. I have it hooked to my small purse. It wouldn't fit inside because I refuse to carry something larger. Especially since I'm heading to the fairgrounds and intend to ride rides. There's a new rollercoaster there this year that I'm very excited to try.

"We should be there in about fifteen minutes, ma'am. There's some cold water if you'd like some. Feel free to take some candy," the young man driving says.

"Thank you," I say quietly. He's probably harmless enough, but I've seen horror stories of drivers drugging things and taking advantage of young women. I may only be twenty-two, but I'm not stupid.

I didn't have a very good home life until I was almost in my teens. I was adopted then by a really nice police officer and his adorable nurse wife. They worked very hard and couldn't have kids of their own. They fostered me when I was finally taken away from my drug addict mom. I was overweight then and had already developed an eating disorder because of how much I'd gotten teased. My foster family chose to adopt me, and I really loved them dearly. I do. I do love them dearly. I always will. They were killed in a plane crash not long ago.

I miss them. I miss them a lot. I've been working hard on my eating disorder and being the best that I can be for them. I finished college for them, even though I wanted to drop out. I got my degree in communications for them. Each day I wake up is a fight, but it's a fight I'll continue to win.

For them.

I keep my eyes on my pepper spray. My small purse is across my body. The pepper spray does give me a sense of safety, but it also gives me comfort. It makes me feel closer to my biker boy somehow.

Boy…

I bite my lip to stifle the chuckle threatening to escape. He's definitely not a boy. He's all man. Every single part of him oozes it. Even his scent screams man. He's definitely leaps and bounds above the boys I've been dating. At least for this date, it doesn't matter if the guy is a dud. I love the fair. I can entertain myself.

When we get there, I start looking around for my date, this time off Hinge. I don't see him, though, and wonder if I should wait. Maybe he already went in. I quickly text him. I don't want to wait outside the gates. It's not really the safest place to be. So, I pay and wait just inside the gates until I hear from him.

It doesn't take long. He tells me he's in the line waiting at the ticket booth near the entrance. I head over there, scanning the crowd, but still don't see him. Finally, someone starts waving at me. He doesn't look anything like his profile pic. He's shorter than he said and definitely more… chunky.

I smile softly. "You must be Mike."

"That's me!" he says as he extends a hand to shake.

I shake his hand and notice that he's actually bigger than I thought. He has a beer gut and is probably only five-seven. His face is pimply. He looks like he's in his late thirties, not the late twenties he said in his profile.

I wait silently with him and get some tickets when we get to the front. When I turn, my so-called date is already walking towards the rides. I shake my head and hurry after him, though I'm completely confused. I've never been on a date where the person was this rude. Rude yes, but this guy seems to take the cake. Literally. All of it.

"We'll go on the Zipper first. And then the Tilt 'a' Whirl. Then there's the ride that looks like you're on a spacecraft. I want to go on that next." He doesn't look at me as he talks. "And after that, we can go play the games they have, but we'll eat first."

"Oh… um… okay. I want to do the rollercoaster, though."

"No way. No rollercoasters."

I blink as I hand tickets to the person taking them when we get to the Zipper. Thankfully, he puts me in my own cart, and when Mike argues, saying we're together, the guy controlling the ride says he has to balance the load. I've never been so grateful. I shoot the guy a smile, and he winks back. I'm really happy he knew I didn't want to be in the same cart.

I'm not so lucky on the Tilt 'a' Whirl or the space ride. I'm put right next to him. That really sucks on the Tilt 'a' Whirl because he crushes me against the side of the stupid pod every time the pod turns my way. When we're finally finished with the rides he wants to go on, I breathe a huge sigh of relief.

The sun is just starting to go down, and Mike takes my hand. "I'm really good at the games. I can win you anything you want."

"Oh. Thank you. I'll meet you there, though. I'm looking forward to the rollercoaster." I pull my hand away, but he grabs it again, more roughly this time.

"We're doing the games next. I don't want to ride the rollercoaster."

"You don't have to. That's okay, but I do." I pull my hand away again, more forcefully, this time, I quickly walk towards the rollercoaster. I'm done with this guy. I'm not meeting anywhere.

"I said I don't want to ride that." He tries to grab me again. My hand wraps around my pepper spray, but I don't end up having to use it.

"Dude. Walk away," a deep, powerful voice I'd know anywhere says. A tall, lean, and muscular body steps protectively in front of me.

Mike's eyes widen comically. He hurries away without saying a single word to me. The man turns towards me. He's tall, definitely over six-feet. He has muscles for days. His jeans fit just right. His black, short sleeve shirt barely contains his muscles. The veins in his arms are accentuated by his many tattoos. His eyes are just as piercing as I remember. His hair is dark and short, but messy. I'm salivating for him. I have the same reaction for him I did last night.

And last night I didn't even see his face or his strong jawline. I only imagined it in the many wet dreams and day fantasies I had about him.

"You okay?" he asks.

"Yeah. Fine. Thanks to you. Again."

He gives me a confused look and raises his eyebrow. "Well, you're welcome."

Do I have the wrong person? Do I just want him to be the sexy biker, but he's really just some random, nice guy who's the same height and build? I clear my throat. "Anyway… um… Thank you."

"You're welcome. Are you going on the rollercoaster?"

I turn towards it, smiling. "Yeah, I've really been looking forward to it." I look up at him as he stands at my side.

"Me too. Wanna go together?"

I smile brightly. "Yeah! For sure!"

We both walk to the line and wait our turn. "So, what's your name?" he asks me after a few minutes of small talk.

"Blair. What about you?"

"You can call me Z."

"Z." I nod. Sounds like a biker name, but I'm really starting to doubt it's the same person. His eyes aren't as intense.

When we finally get to the front of the line, it's dark. I'm even more excited to ride and see the lights of the fair. I wanted to go on the ferris wheel, too, but I don't think I have enough tickets.

"Not enough tickets." The guy controlling the ride hands my tickets back to me. "Need two more."

I shake my head. "Wh-what?" I look down at the five tickets in my hand, then at the guy. "It was five tickets."

"It goes up after dark. It's seven now. Step aside. Next person!" He practically shoves me aside, but Z slides an arm around my waist.

"She's with me. Take her five. I got the two."

"Fine." The guy takes my tickets and the ones Z hands him before he ushers us by. We're seated next to each other on the rollercoaster, and despite how rude the guy was, I'm already overly excited.

"I've been waiting for this for months. Ever since I saw the announcement," I say, smiling wide at Z.

He smiles back, and I melt a little. "Me too." His blue eyes shine, and for a brief moment, before he turns away, I'm certain I see those silver flecks.

My heart stutters.

Is it him? It has to be. I've never seen eyes like his.

I don't have much time to contemplate it. The safety restraint comes down. Two people come down the line on each side of the cars and check the restraint to make sure it's properly working and locked in. My heart starts to beat faster as we take off slowly.

"Here we go," Z says.

"Yay!" I squeal as we start a slow ascent. Once we get to the top, I put my arms up. So does Z.

The drop starts out slow, but we're quickly moving fast. There are screams of excitement and delight as the rollercoaster turns sideways and upside down. As I hoped, the lights from the fair are a spectacular sight from the rollercoaster, but it's the man next to me that truly has my attention. Especially his hand holding mine. I'm not sure when it happened, but I felt that same spark I felt with the biker yesterday. I don't know if my heart is fluttering more because of him or the ride.

Once the ride stops, Z helps me off. He takes me to eat and then to the ferris wheel. He doesn't make a single rude comment. He waits for me. He gives great conversation. I have a really great time with him.

It's only on my way home, I realize I forgot one very important detail.

"Ugh. How could I forget to ask for his number? I suck at this dating thing."

When I reach my door and start to pull out my key, I notice something very odd. I blink a few times. I know when I left earlier, there wasn't a keypad there. It was just a normal lock that was opened with a key. Specifically the key in my hand.

I jump nearly a mile when my phone goes off as I'm backing away from the door. I have to be at the wrong house. I look at the numbers on the house and shake my head. The numbers are mine. They even have the bright pink stickers I put on them to make them pretty and stand out.

I shakily look down at my phone and see a text from a number I've never seen.

> **Unknown: I noticed that not only did you not carry pepper spray, you also didn't have cameras. I got you the spray, but you need those cameras in this neighborhood, so I took the liberty of installing a security system for you while you were at work. The code is 8261. Feel free to change it if you want.**

I blink a few times before looking around. I know deep inside that it's my mysterious biker. I can't see him, but I feel him. I know he's around somewhere… watching me. Most people would fear him. They'd be terrified that he gained access to their home and put up cameras. It's an invasion of privacy if there ever was one.

Am I crazy for feeling safe…?

Chapter Four

Zade

(One Week Later)

I walk my bike up Blair's driveway. It's two in the morning, and there's way too much activity going on in this neighborhood for my liking right now. And it's all from that house just a couple doors from hers. I don't like it. I'm definitely going to be talking to my buddy about that shit. It's way too close to Blair. They can move the house somewhere else.

The past week since I met her has been about as thrilling as that rollercoaster I rode with her. When I first walked up to her at the fair, I was pretty sure she recognized me. She confirmed it when she thanked me and added the word 'again'.

I panicked.

I never panic, but I panicked. I felt like I needed to throw her off my trail and make her think I'm someone else. It worked for a while, but I could tell the second she started to catch on. It was when I took her hand. Still, I took her to eat. I took her on the ferris wheel. I even put her in a Lyft and almost kissed her goodnight. I followed her home, but stayed a good distance away. I saw her look for me, like she could feel my presence, when she saw what I'd installed. I did it while she was at work that day and finished after she left on her date.

I wish I'd gotten to the fairgrounds earlier than I did. That was the second asshole in a row who put hands on her. And the second asshole who ended up in a car accident later that night.

I chuckle to myself as I park my bike. It's easy to cause accidents when you ride a bike. People either swerve right into bikes because they don't see them, or they swerve away from them when they see them coming out of their blind spot. Each of the four guys she's been on a date with this week, two after the fair asshole, has ended up in an accident.

My only regret over this past week is that Blair thinks she's cursed. Which she admitted to me over coffee today at Starbucks where she works. I went in on her break. She recognized me from the fair. I can tell she definitely doesn't think I'm the biker she met anymore.

That's because the biker she met has been relentlessly flirting with her via text. And letting her know that he's watching her. He sees her on these dates. He even got her to cancel the rest of her dates this week. She had one every single night, and I couldn't stand to see it. She belongs with me.

The problem is I've never felt this way about anyone, and I don't know how to handle it. I have a degree in computer science that I never put to use, but it's come in handy with her. I know everything about her. Her age, what school she went to, her GPA, the college she just graduated from with her communications degree. I found her phone number, her parents' names, what they did before they were killed in a plane crash last year. I know she had a rough childhood with a drug addicted whore of a mother. None of it was hard to find out. At least not with my skills.

I keep my helmet on as I walk to her door after I park my bike in her driveway. I punch in the code I gave her and smile when the lock to her door clicks for me. She didn't change it. That tells me she trusts me and secretly hopes I'll show up. I haven't because I wanted to see how she'd react. I wanted to know if she'd miss me. She doesn't know I put cameras in her house just so I could watch her.

Unhinged? Definitely, but this girl is mine. All mine. No one else can have her.

I rearm the alarm and take off my boots and helmet. Tonight's the night. I want her to know who she belongs to, but I'm not ready for her to know me yet. My reasons are many. Once girls figure out who I am and what I do, it's usually game over for me. All they want from me is cash. It's the reason I pursue them now. Not the other way around. If a girl comes up to me, I'm instantly suspicious and usually right.

Blair, though… She's different. I want to be around her. All of the damn time. I know she can handle me for me, but there's so much about me I'm not sure she'd understand. I've done a lot of bad things. Things I've never been caught for and never will. Hard to take someone down when there's no evidence… or witnesses.

I'm not a serial killer. I'm not even a serial stalker. I look at myself as a dark avenger. Kind of like Loki, but darker. He had a soul. Morals. I don't. I see someone messing with someone, I don't think about the consequences it will have on me. I don't think about Heaven or Hell. I don't believe in either of them. An atheist. That's what they call me. Truly, I just don't care. Whatever happens to me when I die, will happen. Nothing I do now or later will help that. Forgive me of my sins? Fuck it. I don't give a damn about judgement day.

I make my way through Blair's house until I reach her bedroom. She has a one floor duplex. I'm glad because I don't want to wake her up with squeaky stairs or doors. I miss her, though, and I want to see her, even though I just did today. What I'm doing is daring as hell, but I need her to know she's mine and only mine.

I still have my helmet liner on. I make sure it's covering my nose and mouth as I reach for the door handle to her room. I hold my breath as I carefully open it. It doesn't make a sound. I quietly let the breath I was holding out as I step inside.

There she is. My girl is just laying there. She doesn't wear anything to bed. One of her perfect feet is sticking out from the blanket. She's laying on her side. Her perky little ass is uncovered. It's like she's just waiting for me. So… fucking… sexy.

I get onto her bed as carefully as I can without waking her up. I just want to look at her. Feel her close. And when I get my fill, I want her to wake up, feel a little fear, and then realize it's me. I know she feels safe with me. I love seeing her expression when she realizes I'm near. It's like she relaxes. I've never experienced anything like it, but I love the feeling.

Blair makes an adorable noise and stretches before she curls right into me, her pretty ass against my thigh. I can't help but groan low. My hand automatically finds her skin and caresses it lightly, loving the way her bare skin feels against my hand. The blanket slips off her, exposing her legs and most of her body. I bite my lip because I can see most of her tits and her pussy. I can see how wet she is.

It would be so easy to slide my fingers into her, testing how wet that glistening pussy actually is. I refrain, and let my fingertips slide up her body instead. I let them move down her back to sexy, round cheeks again. When she arches back into me, I hiss between my teeth.

Her skin is so silky smooth. I know she'd feel like the softest satin wrapped around me.

But not yet.

Tonight, I have other plans.

I allow myself to trace the outline of her tits before I circle her nipple. She arches into me in her sleep. I let my fingers make their way lower… lower… until I circle her belly button. She sighs and smiles softly. Like it's the most natural thing in the world, she falls back into me. Her legs part slightly, one of them sliding over mine.

I keep moving my fingertips down until I'm just above her smooth, glistening pussy. It's like she's waiting for me to take her, and I can't resist the invitation, even though it wasn't in my plans. I slide my middle finger down her wetness until I reach the part of her that my entire being craves. My dick has been rock solid for days, but I ignore it. I'll get off later.

Right now, I need to know if she feels as good as I think she does. I slide my middle finger inside her. She moans and gasps, but her eyes stay closed.

"Good girl," I whisper low in her ear as I move my finger deeper and deeper inside her until I can't go further. "Fuck, you're so wet. Such a dirty girl for daddy, aren't you?" I grin when she bites her lip.

"Mmm…" Her hips thrust to the rhythm of my finger. I had no intention of doing this tonight, but the way she's responding to me makes it impossible to resist. I let her ride it for a few moments before I slide another one inside her.

"Fuck…," I rumble as I watch her.

She bites her lip and before licking it. Her moans and breathing gets heavier. I keep thrusting, letting her use me to get herself to her peak, but I help her along by setting my thumb against her clit. I press and rub it just as I start crooking my fingers inside her, hitting her spot. The perfect spot. The one I know will have her exploding over my fingers in seconds.

Her eyelids start to flutter open as her mouth forms an 'O'. "Mmm...," she moans as her hand moves down. She grabs my wrist as her pussy starts to shudder, gripping my fingers tight.

When her eyes open, I quickly slide my other arm under her head and put my hand over her mouth. She screams as she comes around me. Her hips jerk into me as she orgasms even though she's screaming in fear.

"Ssh..." I whisper as I lean my head down closer to her skin. She smells like vanilla caramel coffee. I'm fucking in love. She's intoxicating. I can't get enough of her. "I got you, baby," I rumble.

My voice instantly calms her. Her orgasm rocks her, even as she starts to come down. I thrust slower and slower until I feel her completely relax. She watches me in wonder. I can tell she wants to be afraid, but she isn't. That has to feel off to her. Abnormal.

She keeps one hand around my wrist as I pull my fingers out of her. I keep my hand cupped around her pussy like I'm protectively guarding what belongs to me. She pants into my hand. Her other hand is around my other wrist. I slowly remove my hand from her mouth. If she screams, which I don't think will happen, I'll slap my hand right down on her mouth again.

"Wh-what's... h-happening...?" she asks. Her hand is still around my wrist as I trail my fingers down her throat and to her chest. Her heart is rapidly beating.

"Claiming what's mine," I say simply. "You. You're mine." I nuzzle her cheek with my nose. "Breathe, baby."

She takes a deep, shaky breath. She's slightly on her side, but she turns towards me. With trembling hands, she slowly lets go of me. Her hands move to my chest. She spreads both of her palms over my heart. Using me to calm her, like she did the first day I met her, she slowly starts to become tranquil once more.

"No more dates. You're mine. You're done looking for love."

"No more dates," she murmurs. "Yours..."

"Good girl."

Before long, she's asleep once more. I take a few more minutes to breathe her in before I gently tuck her in and get out of the bed. I walk to the door and take one last look at her before I close her door. As I walk down the hall towards the front door, I pull up my mask and stick my fingers in my mouth. I suck her sweetness off them with a low groan.

Tonight was just a taste, but I can't wait to devour her the way she deserves to be.

Soon…

Chapter Five

Blair

(One Week Later)

How *dare* he? How DARE he?

How dare he break into my house, scare the hell out of me, make me come harder than I've ever come in my life, and then make me feel safe? How dare he claim me and forbid me from dating, and then literally just ghost me for an entire week?

Screw him! I scream to myself. *Screw him and his stupid hands. Screw him and his stupid eyes. Screw him and his stupid claim!*

I nearly throw my phone into my small purse. I struggle to zip the dumb thing as I storm into the restaurant, schooling my face. I don't want my date to see me so pissed off. That's not a good first impression, and I'm way better than that.

Unlike *some* people.

I push the sexy biker out of my head as I'm shown to my date's table. The man smiles up at me. He looks just like his profile pic. That's a good start. Tall, blond, brown-eyed. The perfect, sexy surfer boy vibe, even though we don't have surfing anywhere near Spark, Nevada. He looks like he has a good body. A muscular runner's body. Someone who probably works out, but never does the same thing every time.

"Hey, I hope you don't mind I ordered an app. I came right here from work and was pretty hungry," the guy says. Max. That's his name.

"No. Not at all." I smile as he stands. He pulls my chair out like a true gentleman. It's shocking, but I smile and take my seat. He pushes my chair in. "Thank you," I say as he sits.

"Of course. Wow. Forgive me, but you're as beautiful as your pic. Don't see that often."

My eyes widen. "Oh my god, right? It's crazy. I don't understand the purpose of lying. If you're gonna meet up, the person is going to see you for what you are."

Max shakes his head. "Man, you're not kidding." He takes a chip and dips it in the spinach dip this restaurant is known for. My mouth waters. "Feel free to eat some," Max says with a grin.

I smile brightly and immediately feel at ease. Maybe this date won't suck. Maybe something will come of it. A second date at least.

That'll teach him, I grumble in my head.

As our date goes on, I find myself liking Max more and more. He's funny. Smart. He has a good job in finance. The guy, on the surface, really seems down to earth and real. He even likes Eminem. To me, if someone doesn't like Eminem, or at least respects him, it's a red flag. His talent is undeniable.

The rest of the date goes well. I even make a second date. I'm all smiles when I walk out of the restaurant with Max. We're laughing as we wait for my Lyft, but that laughter quickly dies when I hear a very familiar engine rumble.

As if in slow motion, I turn towards the sound and see the biker, my biker, stopping and parking at the curb next to me. I hear nothing more. Time stops. My breath catches. Max is saying something, but I don't know what. I wouldn't be able to say even if I was taking a quiz about it that my life depended on. My eyes are glued to the biker. The one who hasn't made any contact with me for an entire week.

The one who *claimed me* as his.

And then left me alone.

The more I watch him, the more angry I become. As he gets off his bike with all of the grace and sexiness in the world, I plaster a smile on my face and look up at Max. I turn towards him and gently take his arm.

"I really had a great time with you."

"It's been a real pleasure, Blair. I'm looking forward to the next one," Max says low, sex oozing from his deep voice.

"There won't be a next one," the biker growls, taking my arm and pulling me forcefully away from Max. He spins me around as he shoves me behind him, placing himself in front of me and Max.

"What the hell!" I shout. I try to move back around him, but he easily holds me back with one arm. I thought Max was tall at six feet, but this biker is easily six feet five. He towers over Max. He's built better than Max. My mind drifts to Z, but I really don't think they're the same person.

"I said no dates," he growls low as he looks back at me. He's still wearing his helmet but his visor is up. His blue eyes look like they're on fire. He's pissed.

"Let me go!" I shout, but he doesn't. His grip on my arm tightens as he turns back to Max.

"Dude, what the fuck? Get off her!" Max moves towards him, but the biker pushes him back. Hard. Max stumbles, but doesn't fall.

"Get on the bike, Blair," the biker commands.

I grab his arm and try to spin out of his grip, but it doesn't work. "Let me go! What are you doing?" I hit his upper arm, but it feels like I'm hitting metal. His muscles are solid.

"Get off her! What's your problem, man?" Max tries to grab me away, but the biker punches him in the face. He screams out as he stumbles back. Blood instantly covers his nose and hands.

"Ah!" I scream, suddenly terrified, even though I know instinctually I'm safe. Even still, a fight instinct kicks in, and I try to shove him off me, but he only turns and grabs me around the waist.

"Stop it! Did he fucking tell you he's suspected of multiple rapes? Get on the goddamn bike, Blair!"

I immediately stop fighting him and do what he says. My eyes feel like they're about to pop out of my head. I'm starting to hyperventilate. *Oh my god, what?* I scream internally. That could've been me! I could've been his next victim! *I'm so stupid!*

We've drawn a crowd. Someone is on the phone. Others are taking pics of the bike. Others seem to be recording the entire situation. I try to get on the bike, but I'm struggling because I'm both shaking, and I'm short.

The biker squats in front of me, his back facing me. "Grab on."

I do what he says because I'm too shaken up to do anything else. I grip his shoulders and let him lift me like he's piggy-backing me. I wrap my legs around his waist. He swings a leg effortlessly over his bike and sits, allowing me to easily settle behind him.

"I… don't…" I struggle to find a place for my legs and feet. "I've… never been on a bike…"

He reaches back and puts a peg down on each side of his bike. "Put your feet on the pegs." He turns towards me. I do what he says as he takes his helmet off. "Put this on." He has that helmet liner on, so I still can't see his face. "It'll be too big, but it'll give you some protection."

Without a word, I put the helmet on. He helps with the chin strap before he puts the visor down. He turns around and starts the bike. I hear yelling and turn to see someone running towards us.

"Hey! The cops are coming! You can't leave!" The woman has short blond hair, and is wearing way too much makeup.

"Watch me. Hold on tight, baby."

"Where?" I fumble to find grips, but he reaches behind himself and grabs my hands. He pulls them so my arms wrap around his midsection. My front is flush to his back. "Lean when I do. Don't fight. Hold the fuck on."

Just as the woman gets close, the biker guns it away from the curb and takes off. The last thing I see before my attention is wholly diverted is Max being helped up by someone, but he isn't what my attention is on. It's not even the biker and how good his hard body feels against mine.

It's the cops that chase us.

"Oh my god!" I shriek. "Cops!"

The biker says nothing but I can feel him pick up speed. The powerful bike feels like it's flying as it rumbles between my bare thighs. My dress is definitely showing things it shouldn't, but there's nothing I can do about it. I don't dare let go of him.

I close my eyes and feel his every movement. I mold myself to his body so when he leans, I do. When he moves his body forward, mine moves with him. I can hardly hear the sirens over the roar of the bike's engine, but they seem to be getting further and further away. I don't know how fast we're going, but it feels like it must be over a hundred.

I don't know how long we ride, but by the time he starts slowly down, I've almost forgotten my reasons for being mad at him. I keep my eyes closed until he comes to a stop. I feel him straighten. He removes my interlocked hands from around his waist before he gets off the bike.

"You're not allowed to wear that dress when we're riding again. People can see what belongs to me," he says, his voice low and demanding.

And just like that, the infuriation reaches a level that scares the hell out of me. "What's yours?" I laugh manically. "What's yours? Yet you haven't talked to me in a week. Haven't made any contact at all." I try to get off the bike. "Show up in a mask. Refuse to show your face." I nearly fall, but he catches me. "Give me the best orgasm of my life, yet never allow me to see your stupid face!" He helps me off the bike and helps me take off the helmet. Once it's off, I push him off me and stomp towards my house. "I'm crazy! I have to be! Who sits here waiting for some unknown, helmeted biker to sweep her off her feet? Who sits here and believes what he says about her being his?" I punch in my code and spin on my heel towards him. "I'm not doing this anymore! Leave me alone!"

"I couldn't do that even if I wanted to."

"I bet Max isn't even suspected of anything, is he? You're just a jealous stalker!" I try to slam the door in his face, but it doesn't work. "Ah!" I scream when he shoves it open.

"Do you think I'd fucking lie to you? After all I've already fucking done for you?" He pushes me into my house, keeping his hands at my waist. My eyes are wide. My heart races. He kicks the door shut. "After I've done everything I can to fucking protect you? Did you ask me why I was gone for a fucking week? Or just assume it's because I didn't want to be here?" He slams me against my wall.

"Ah!" I scream again. I shove him back, but he doesn't budge. Instead, he crowds closer and grips me just underneath my ass. He lifts me. I have no choice but to wrap my legs around his waist to keep from falling as he pins me between his body and the wall.

"Did you honestly think I didn't want you? After the risk I took to be with you? Breaking into your house at fucking two in the morning?

Installing that security system in the first fucking place? Saving you from how many bad dates? From a fucking rapist?" He rips off his helmet liner, revealing himself for the first time.

My eyes widen, and I gasp before promptly passing out…

Chapter Six

Zade

"Is this what you wanted, Blair? Is this -" I cut myself off when Blair's eyes widen before falling closed as she goes limp in my arms. "Oh fuck!" I drop my helmet liner and carry her to her couch. I lay her down and drop to my knees next to her. "Fuck, Blair. Wake up, baby." I gently slap her cheeks. "Come on, sweet girl. Wake up for me."

It takes her several moments, but she starts to come out of it. "Mmm…" She shakes her head as her eyes flutter open.

"Come on, baby. Wake up for me."

"Mmm…" She leans into my hand as I cup her cheek. "Z…?" she asks hesitantly as her eyes flutter closed again.

"Yeah, baby. Z. Zade. My name is Zade."

"Zade…," she murmurs. She reaches up and gently grips my wrist. She nuzzles her cheek into my palm. "I don't understand what's happening," she whispers.

"I'll explain. I promise. Let me get you some water."

Her hand falls to the bed. "Mmm…" Her eyes close. "Okay…"

I battle with myself to wake her up again but choose to get the water first. Her trust in me is truly astounding and grounding. The fact that she didn't wake up screaming at me really goes a long way in showing me just how deep that trust goes. If she knew my past, she'd probably run screaming from me. I'd never allow that, and that's where I become a bad guy. That's where I get dark.

Because I wouldn't let her run from me. I'd chase her. I'd catch her. I'd fuck her right at the spot I found her just to remind her who she belongs to. And then I'd drag her back to my house and lock her inside it. I'm no prince. She's my beauty. I'm her beast. She'll understand one day all of the things I've done for her; all of the things I will do for her.

I walk back to her room with a bottle of water. I've done things I'll never tell a soul. I might be a millionaire biker with a huge social media presence, but there's a lot more to me that people will never know. I live in a shadow world with zero light.

Blair…

She's my light.

I kneel next to her and place the water bottle on the end table next to the couch. I help her sit up, and then I sit on the couch where her head was. "Take a sip," I say as I grab the bottle and keep her sat up. I take the cap off and bring the bottle to her lips. She grabs the bottle in her tiny hands and tries to gulp. "No. I said sip." I move the bottle away. She turns her head towards me and nods. Like a good girl, she sips.

Once she's done, I set the bottle on her end table again and help her lay down with her head in my lap. She turns so her face it's towards me, and her mouth is inches away from my dick. I suck in a sharp breath when she nuzzles her head into it and closes her eyes.

Fuck, she's the only one who has the ability to make me hard as fucking granite without doing anything. All she has to do is look at me, and I'm ready to sink myself deep into her pussy and give her the pounding she deserves.

And damn, does my sexy little girl deserve it.

"I'm sorry…," she whispers.

I feel her lips against my length, but she's comfortable. I'm not making her move no matter how hard I get. "For what?" I ask, knowing the answer.

"For not listening to you. I just… I didn't hear from you… I didn't have any way to get a hold of you. I thought…" She sighs. "I don't know."

"You thought I wasn't coming back. That I was being an asshole and ghosting you."

She nods, nuzzling into me more. "Yes, sir." She sounds exhausted.

"I know I played a part in this. I should've been better. I got called away. I didn't contact you. I should've. That's my fault. But don't ever go against my orders again, Blair. Next time, it could mean your life."

She looks up at me confused. I look down at her with as much seriousness as I can muster. She watches me, like she's trying to figure out if I'm being dramatic or not. There's nothing dramatic about it. I'm not just a biker. Not just the mystery behind my brand. I don't just have a degree in computer science.

I've pissed off a lot of people. I've used my unique set of skills to take a lot of dangerous people down. I've leaked sensitive information about politicians to very high offices. Vigilante? Sure. Some can call me that. But vigilantes have a soul. I don't. I'm only kind to those I care about. And those I care about can be counted with two fingers. Myself.

And Blair.

I'd burn the world down if it meant keeping her safe and by my side.

As if she finally understands, she looks down again and lays her head back in my lap. She nuzzles right back into my dick, and I can't help the groan I let out.

"Am I really yours?" she asks me after a few moments of silence.

"Yes," I say without hesitation. "I don't want anyone else. I want you. Giving you up isn't an option. I'd follow you to the ends of the universe and drag you back by your hair."

She chuckles. "Don't make promises you can't keep. Apparently, I'm a walking red flag."

I raise an eyebrow. "Who the fuck told you that? That asshole from today?"

"No…" She shifts and lays on her back. I lay my arm across her middle, just underneath her perfect, round tits. "He was actually really nice. It's why I was so surprised when you said what you did about him. It's just other people making me believe things I know in my head aren't true. I'm too clingy. I'm fat. Max… well, he was opposite of all of that."

I reach into my pocket and pull out my phone. Within seconds, I have information up on him that she'd never be able to find with a simple search. I hand her my phone. "Scroll."

She takes my phone and does as she's told. I hear a few grumbles and scoffs, but other than that, she's relatively quiet while she reads. There are pages and pages of police reports of women who have accused him of sexual assault dating all the way back to his college years at Yale. Just when she thinks she's done, she'll hit his sealed records from when he was a senior in high school.

The entire reason he hasn't gotten in trouble or spent time in jail is because of his father, who is a very top notch attorney. His mom left his dad when Max was eighteen. I wonder why, but not really. I have the answer to that question in there, too. Officially, it's irreconcilable differences, but reading deeper in the paperwork, it's spelled out. She left because of what her son did, and the fact that her husband defended him both personally and legally.

"The evidence against him is overwhelming… Why is he not behind bars?" Blair finally asks.

"Because of who his father is. He's good at what he does. He got him off every time by proving the sex was totally consensual. Can't put such a good, respectable man behind bars when the girl he was with just regretted what happened and decided to make up a story."

"Well, okay, but there's pages upon pages of assaults here. So much evidence."

"All great actors."

"All twenty-three of them? And that poor high school cheerleader."

"I'm with you, honey. But that's the argument. He's a good guy. They are all sluts."

She shivers as she gives me back my phone. "I'm sorry. I'm sorry I didn't listen to you. Trust you. I do trust you." She looks up at me and nibbles her lip. "Why? Why do I trust you? I barely know you."

I gently run a rough thumb over her lower lip. "There's no explanation sometimes." I cup her cheek. The hole where my heart should be fills up a little with something warm and fuzzy. I'd be pissed off if I wasn't head over heels for this girl. "Sometimes, it's just an inconceivable pull between two souls. There's no rhyme or reason. It just is."

She nods slowly as her eyes slowly close. "That makes sense."

I run my fingers through her hair. "You tired?"

Blair nods. "Honestly, I think everything just hit me all at once…" She pauses before opening her eyes and meeting mine. "Where were you this last week? Am I allowed to ask that?"

"You can ask me anything you want. I was called away to some meetings. Brand stuff. I have a big following on social media for my bike stuff, and I have a lot of brand deals and my own clothing and gear line. I had a lot of stuff going on, but the reason I disappeared is because I got a call at four in the morning about a factory I use in Texas being burned to the ground. There were two workers there. One of them believed it was the owner of the factory. Well, not believe. The other worker there knew. She saw. She's a single mom. Works hard for her son. She's the one who called me. Good friend of mine."

"And you had to go and deal with that…?" She looks at me a little skeptical, and I don't blame her. I'm leaving a lot of stuff out.

Against my better judgement, I decide to tell her everything. "I have a computer science degree. She called because she knew I could find a link to the cameras before the cops could. And I don't need a warrant. I can get anything I want before the evidence is tainted by someone else. And I did. I gave it to the police with her name. She saw everything that happened. She just needed proof. The cameras backed her story."

"I understand. And it speaks to your character. Protective. Caring."

She turns back onto her side and snuggles into me, her face right against my cock once more. Fuck me, this girl is going to be the death of me, but if this is what she needs, this is what she gets.

So while she's burrowed face first into me, I rub a hand up and down her back and get comfortable. I wouldn't dream of moving her. Not when she looks so peaceful.

This is how I want her to be forever.

This peaceful.

And I'll take anyone's life to make sure it happens.

Chapter Seven

Blair

I jerk awake and groan when I get a face full of something hard. Hard fabric… metal… and god only knows what else. Probably a steel rod.

"Where am I?" I grumble.

"In your house. On the couch," a deep voice says. It sends shivers down my spine and makes me smile.

"Zade…," I whisper. I stretch and slowly blink my eyes open. "How long have I been out?"

"A couple hours, but considering you haven't slept very well this past week, I understand why. You needed me to feel safe sleeping, and I wasn't around."

My heart skips several beats, but the idea of him blaming himself for my poor sleeping habits. I look up at him. "It's not your fa-"

He presses a finger to my lips. "Shh… It's my fault. I wasn't here. Your mind spiraled many different directions. I don't blame you for the direction it went. But I'm here now. I'm not going anywhere."

He runs his fingers through my hair, and I relax into him. I take a deep breath, breathing him in, before realizing just where my head is. "Oh my god! I'm so sorry!" I launch myself up, but his large hand at the back of my head keeps me firmly in place.

"Why are you sorry?"

My eyes widen. "Because I'm face to face with your…" I trail off and just stare. The outline of his cock leaves absolutely nothing to the imagination. He's hard and big. Thick.

"My…" The smirk in his voice makes me blush.

"The snake in your pants." I giggle.

He laughs. "Oh, baby. You have no idea." It twitches, and I squeak.

"Why was that so hot?" I ask him, rubbing my thighs together, hopefully subtly enough that he doesn't notice.

"Maybe…" He lets his hand fall from my hips to between my thighs. "Well, no. Not maybe. Probably. Probably because you want it so bad."

I giggle, then trace the outline with my tongue. When I reach his tip, I nip it. He makes some kind of a noise that's between a growl and a groan. It's so hot. Especially when his dick twitches again. It's like it's telling me to come get it.

I bite my lip and look up at him, silently asking for permission. He gives me a sexy smirk, his eyes darkening, and I take that as my invitation. I shift so I can undo his black, leather belt, followed by popping the button of his jeans. He lets me do it, rubbing his hand on my hip after he pushes the skirt of my dress up. His warm hand against my skin gives me goosebumps, and I breathe a sigh of pleasure out as I slowly unzip his zipper.

Once I have it down, my eyes widen. He's not wearing any underwear. I look up at him again to make sure it's okay. He gives me an encouraging smile as his fingertips grip my hip a little tighter. His other hand has my hair wrapped around it. It feels so good. So natural. Like this is how it's meant to be.

I slowly slide one finger along his base. He definitely manscapes. I bite my lip. I want nothing more than to taste him. He's tasted me. It's only fair, right?

I lick my lips as I push my hand into his jeans. My fingertips close around his thick length, and I gasp. It's like holding a satin encased steel rod in my hand. I squeeze lightly as I pull his length out of his jeans. Once more, I look up at him. I want to lick him so bad, but I'm not doing a thing without his command. I need it.

His tongue darts over his sexy lips. He pushes my head towards his cock. It's at least ten inches, and I know I have no chance of taking it all in my mouth, but I'm damn well going to try. If I choke, I'll die happy.

When my lips reach his tip, my tongue slips out and slides around the head of his dick.

"Mmm… fuck…," Zade moans. He pushes my head a little closer, and I close my eyes as I savor him.

"Yummy," I say when I pull back.

"Yeah? Suck me, then." He pushes my head closer again.

This time, I take him as deeply into my mouth as I can while wrapping both hands around his dick. I don't have more than a couple of inches in before my gag reflex sets off. I pull back a little and suck him hard. I revel in his eyes rolling back as his head drops back. He tugs my hair to pull me away before he pushes me down again.

I let my body melt into his and let him do as he pleases with me. I let him control the pace. I let him control how deeply I take him. And when his hand falls between my thighs once more, I part my legs for him. He rubs his thumb on the outside of my panties as I suck him. He doesn't give me time to swallow, so spit drips from my lips and down his shaft.

I use my hands to stroke his cock so every part of his length that I can't reach with my mouth is getting attention. His hand palms my pussy. He rubs, making me moan, but when two of his long fingers slide into my wetness after pushing my panties aside, I scream. Since he's controlling what my head does, the scream is around his dick. He jerks into my mouth and thrusts his fingers hard, deep, and fast, keeping up with the pace he's set for my mouth.

It takes seconds for my greedy pussy to want to orgasm. I try closing my legs around his hand to let him know what's about to happen, but he uses his arm to push them open again. He looks down at what his hand is doing, and I blush furiously.

"Such a good pussy, taking daddy's fingers."

I turn a much darker red as my thighs tremble. I feel like there's an actual earthquake about to happen. "Mmm!" I scream again around his cock as I look up at him.

"You're gonna come. And you're gonna swallow mine," he rumbles dominantly.

"Mmm!" It's something between a moan and scream as that earthquake hits at a ten. I nearly rocket off the couch. Somehow, I don't. I keep stroking and sucking. I feel him getting thicker for me. I taste the salty, tangy taste of his precome.

"Ah, Blair!" he roars as he releases a jetstream of come in my mouth. His hips jerk just as mine do.

It's so sexy watching him orgasm that all I can do is obey his every wish and command and swallow. I slow my strokes just as he does his thrusts. I swallow all he has to give.

"Mmm…" I pull back after licking him clean. His fingers are still buried deep inside me. He pulls them out slowly, and I moan at the loss, but watching him suck me off them is so sexy.

I slowly sit up. I can feel the fire in my cheeks, the visual sign of how embarrassed I am for what I'm about to do. I straddle him. His still hard length is standing at attention just for me. Zade grips my hips. Delirious with lust, I lean in, intending to kiss him.

Instead, after a loud blast, I find myself jumping off him like he shoved me. He stands and takes my hand, pushing me behind him.

"What was that?" I ask, barely above a whisper. "Did I imagine that?"

"No. No, baby, I heard it, too." Zade buttons and zips his pants as his eyes dart around, looking for the source of the loud noise we just heard. He quickly buckles his belt.

"That sounded like an explosion."

"I know. I know, baby." He keeps one hand on my hip as he moves, backing me up. "Get away from windows."

"Yes, sir." I take his hand and start leading him towards the bathroom. It's the only room in the house without a window.

Another explosion seems to shake all the walls, and I scream. I try to dive behind the counter in my kitchen, but Zade stops me. He hauls me against his body and presses my mouth against his chest to silence me. I squeeze my eyes closed, but instantly start panicking when I smell smoke. I grip his shirt and look up at him, wild eyed.

He's not looking at me, though.

His eyes are glued to something, but he doesn't let me look.

"We need to go. Now." He takes my hand and leads me to the door. "Put your shoes on."

I hurriedly do as he says. I grab a jacket and put it on as he cautiously opens the door. Most of his body is blocking my view, but what I see makes me sick.

I put both hands up to my mouth to stifle the scream…

Chapter Eight

Zade

"Ah!" Blair screams behind me. It sounds muffled. I don't need to see her to know that she's screaming into her hands. My bike is up in flames, and so is the wall of her garage. Which likely means the front of her garage is also aflame.

"Good fucking girl," I rumble. I don't want her scream to alert anyone who might be watching. Like the guy in the leather jacket who's lighting a bottle on fire right now. He meets my eyes and gives me a disgusting and manic grin. "Max," I growl under my breath. I don't want Blair to hear me.

"What?" she squeaks.

My eyes darken when Max throws the bottle right at the front door. I slam it and push Blair back as I turn towards her, my back to the door. "Close your eyes," I whisper as I push her head against my chest. I spin us around the corner and use a wall for cover. I cover her with my body.

Another explosion forces another scream from Blair. I know the front door exploded in a hail of flames.

Thinking of the layout of her house as quickly as I can, I try and figure out an escape plan. I know her keys are hanging up near the door where my leather jacket is. Her garage connects to her house. The door is just on the other side of this wall. I can get her keys and my jacket while she gets that door open. I know the garage isn't fully engulfed.

It can't be.

Fuck. I can't let her open that door herself.

"Okay. Here's what we're going to do. You're not moving a single fucking inch. I'm getting your keys and my jacket. We're getting in your car and taking off. I'm driving. Understand?" I look down at her. She nods.

Quickly, I let her go. I glance around the wall. Just as I thought, the door is engulfed, but it hasn't fallen. Yet. That gives me protection. I don't know if Max has a gun waiting for us or not, but I don't want to chance it. I grab my coat and her keys. I see the purse she carries to work and grab it, hoping it has her ID, at least, in it.

I take her hand and pull her to the garage door. I touch the door and handle. It's warm, but not hot, so I cautiously open it. When no flames rush through, I glance around the door and see just what I expected. The wall near the door, as well as the garage door itself, is on fire. The car, a newer Ford Mustang, purple of all colors, is sitting untouched.

I've never been so grateful to see it. That's our escape. Our ticket the fuck out of here. She drives, but she always takes a Lyft or Uber to her dates. It's an incredible way to protect herself. I'll have to tell her how smart that is later. Right now, I need to get us out of here.

"Ah!" Blair screams again as she grabs my arm just as the front window shatters. Seconds later, her living room is on fire.

"Time to go." I pull her towards her car. I open the passenger side door and push her inside.

To her credit, she's already scrambling so the shove doesn't knock her off balance. The second her feet are inside, I'm slamming the door. I run to the other side and jump in. After I quickly adjust the seat, she's over a foot shorter than I am, I put the keys in the ignition and adjust the mirror. I need them or I wouldn't bother. I put my seatbelt on and make sure hers is on. I start the car and slam it into gear.

I floor the pedal and rocket out of the garage, praying like hell the car will hold out and go through the flimsy aluminum door without the entire bumper coming off. I keep backing up until I feel us hit the street. My glare meets that of Max, who's lighting another Molotov cocktail.

Whipping the wheel to the left, the car spins. I slam on the brakes and put the car in drive before flooring the gas once more and taking off.

No way Max is going to catch up to us in that piece of shit red Camry I think he drives, but I keep my attention on my mirrors to make sure he's not following as I speed to the freeway.

Blair doesn't say a word.

Once we hit the freeway, I breathe a sigh of relief, but I don't drop my attention from the mirrors. I do glance at my scared and shaking girl, though. I reach over and put a hand on her thigh. She's clutching my jacket and her purse to her chest, but uses one hand to grip my hand. She stares straight ahead.

"I know things are moving fast with us, Blair," I start, "but I need you to know that I really do care about you. It started as obsession, I'll be honest, but it turned into a lot more than that very quickly for me. Now, I'll do anything for you and not blink an eye."

She gives my hand a squeeze and nods but still says nothing. Understanding she needs to process the bullshit that just happened, I keep my hand on her thigh and rub my thumb in slow circles on her bare skin.

After about thirty minutes of driving, I finally reach the road to my house. It's one of the things, other than bikes, that I've splurged on. I can't wait to show her, but I also know she'll likely be thrown off and have a lot of questions.

Questions that I find myself, for once, happy to answer.

It's so different with her. Everything is so different. I'm not the best guy. I have a very dark side. I didn't start this whole thing with her on the up and up, but fuck… I feel things for her. Things I've never felt for anyone else. It was instant lust, but it grew very quickly into something more. I couldn't stop the firenado if I tried. It exploded and took off, incinerating everything in its path except the two of us.

Jury's still out on that. It might destroy us yet, but it's going to be fun while it lasts.

I pull into my driveway and drive a bit before we get to my circular driveway. My house is two stories and sprawls over seventy-five hundred square feet. I have an outdoor pool and jacuzzi as well as indoor jacuzzi. In my master bathroom, there's a large shower with several different spray heads. The house is way too big for one person, but I don't care. It's mine. Everything in it and on my property is bought and paid for. I don't like owing anyone anything.

"I'm sorry about your bike," Blair whispers. She's hugging herself, and I hate everything about that.

I park in front of my house and squeeze her thigh. "I can get another one. The bike isn't as important as you and your life."

She nods as she starts to get out of the car, still clutching my jacket and her purse like it's her lifeline. I can't blame her. She lost everything back there. Her entire life. I'm sure the people next door to her did, too. I make a mental note as I climb out of the car to check and make sure that the other people have their hotel stay and accommodations paid for as long as they need it.

I hurry to her side of the car and help her out. I quickly assess the damage to her car and see it's pretty much totaled. The back bumper is gone. The frame is all crushed near the rear, driver's side. I'm surprised we got here as quickly as we did without having other issues because it looks like there might even be a fuel leak.

All things I'll deal with. I don't want her worrying about any of this. I put an arm around her and lead her inside. I'll give her the tour later. I know she's not up for it. Fuck… I'm not even up for it. Once we're inside, I secure the alarm and turn to her. I lift her in my arms. She curls into me, and all I can think of is how I need to protect her at all costs. Her pain physically hurts me. I'll never be able to walk away from her.

I carry her directly to my master bedroom and to the bathroom. I sit on the edge of the jacuzzi tub with her in my lap and start running the water. She needs time to relax and decompress, and I know the smell of the smoke is a very powerful reason she's staying locked in her mind.

Once I have the temperature right and bubbles in, I help her out of her clothes. She barely acknowledges what I'm doing, and that scares me. I expect her to be in shock, but it's almost like she's numb. Like she's going through the motions, but she's not really here.

I help her in the bath after I shut off the water. She settles into the heat and bubbles and closes her eyes with an adorable sigh. It's the kind of sound that lets me know she's going to be okay. She's tough. She just needs to process in her own way.

"I'll leave you to relax, baby. I'll just be in the bedroom."

Without opening her eyes, she reaches for me. "Stay…," she whispers, her voice broken. "Just for a little while…"

I can't leave her. I squeeze her palm and sit on the edge of the tub once more. I'd give up everything I have to make her happy again. To make her feel safe and protected.

Fucking loved.

It's so obvious to me that's why she goes out with these douchefucks. She needs to feel loved. She needs to feel everything that I know I can give her. Everything I will give her.

As soon as I make the asshole who made her feel unsafe and took everything from her regret ever being born.

Chapter Nine

Blair

(Two Weeks Later)

I breathe a sigh of relief after hanging up with my boss. Since the fire that Max started took everything, I haven't been able to work. It took me a couple of days to really come down from the shock. When I did, I cried in Zade's arms for hours upon hours. It was almost like something inside me just broke. Something that could never be fixed.

And then Zade fixed it. He did the impossible and truly healed me. Put me back together. He made me realize that I'm stronger than I realize. That as long as I'm breathing, I can get through anything.

The truth is that I can get through anything… as long as I have him.

Once I was feeling up to it, Zade gave me a tour of his home. It's just as beautiful inside as it is outside. It truly fits him. I've gotten to know him more and more each day, and everything I learn about him, I see it somehow incorporated into his home. His darkness can be seen in all of the dark furniture. The brightness I see in him that he tries so hard to hide is in the light that streams through the windows into the rooms.

But my favorite is how down to earth and classic Zade is. That can be found in every edge, every corner, of his home. His home shows his heart. To everyone who walks in here, they'll feel the cold and darkness, but to me, I see how every atom of his home exudes how much he cares for it.

I walk from Zade's bedroom down the stairs. "Zade?" I call. I want to let him know that I quit Starbucks. I haven't been able to go in without having a panic attack at being away from him. Even when he offered to stay with me, I had one leaving the house.

It's safe here.

When I don't see him in the kitchen, den, living room, or his office, I pause. My heart starts racing a little. I don't like the idea of being alone, but I take a deep breath. Zade wouldn't leave me alone. If he had to, he'd tell me. We'd have a plan.

"Garage," I whisper to myself. The garage is Zade's happy place. He has several bikes and a couple of cars in there, including the new Mustang he bought to replace my totaled one. It's purple, just like my other one, but it's brand new. He loves everything in that garage, but he has a favorite.

I head for the garage and quietly open the door. It's connected to the house, so I don't need to go outside. I lean against the door and bite my lip. Zade is wearing a pair of tight black jeans and a black t-shirt that shows off his muscles and his tattoos. He has a lot of them all up and down his arms, but it's the dagger on his chest that really gets me hot. I don't know why. I won't pretend to understand that any more than I understand what he's doing with his bike right now.

It's brand new. He just bought it. It's another black Kawasaki Ninja ZX-10R Supersport to replace the one that Max set on fire. He's always tinkering with something on it, but he loves it, so I never say anything.

Especially since he always makes it up to me. Whether it's his fingers, tongue, or my new favorite thing, his dick making me incapable of walking for a while, he always makes me happy. He's so attentive to me and my needs. I didn't know relationships could be this good. Maybe it's our age difference. He's thirty-four. Or maybe it's just that he's a man and not a boy. He knows how to treat people, women especially.

"You just gonna stare at me? Or are you gonna come over and be my eye candy while I finish up?"

I giggle at Zade's voice suddenly breaking my thoughts. I walk to him. "You just looked so good. I couldn't help it."

"Well, guess you get to return the favor." He finishes adjusting something before he puts his tool down. He wipes his hands on his jeans as he stands and looks me up and down.

I blush as I stop in front of him. "You're sexy when you work on things I don't understand."

He grins. "And you're sexy when you pretend to understand, but I think you're more sexy in those tiny shorts and sexy as fuck, barely there tank." He steps closer and pulls the spaghetti strap of my pink tank top. "Who said you could wear this?"

I giggle again. "My boyfriend. He likes when I wear pink."

Zade steps closer, his hands dropping to my hips. He pulls me closer with a possessive growl. "Well, you're mine now. Too bad for your boyfriend. Bikers do it better."

I laugh because I can't help it as I hook my thumbs through the belt loops of his jeans. "They do, don't they?"

"They steal."

"And lie."

"And fuck."

I laugh. "Steal good girls and make them bad. Lie them down, and fuck them."

Zade grins. "Now you got it." He grips my ass and lifts me. I squeal and laugh as I wrap my legs around his waist and arms over his shoulders. He claims my mouth with his as he gets on his bike.

I furrow my brows when he pulls away and sits down. "This is an odd way to ride a bike."

"Yeah. But we're not riding the bike. You're about to ride the biker, though."

My eyes widen. "On the bike?"

"Fuck yes." His hands grip my hips and pull me down the gas tank until my front is flush with him. I can feel his hard length between my legs. I'm already getting wet for him.

I hang onto his shoulders as he trails my body with his fingers, sending chills up my spine and giving me goosebumps everywhere he touches. He leans forward and kisses me between my breasts, and I gasp. His touch always does that to me. It's always like the first time.

I kiss his neck and hear him undoing his belt. I inhale sharply because I know what that means for me. While my lips still against his neck, Zade lifts his hips and tugs his jeans down enough to free his impressive length. I tremble because I know how good it feels. I'll never get enough. Being tangled up with him is my favorite thing to do.

He doesn't undo my button. He doesn't unzip my shorts. He doesn't pull them down. Instead, I feel his hands slide up my legs. They move to my inner thighs. His fingers push aside my shorts and panties. Just as the cool air in the garage hits my naked skin, he's pushing his dick deep inside me.

"Oh… fuck… Oh, Zade." My eyes roll back, and I arch into him.

"Such a pretty girl." He pushes my tank top up, revealing my naked and braless breasts, as he lays me back over his bike. My nails scratch lightly down his arms as I close my eyes. He thrusts deep and hard, moving his hands down my body, flicking my nipples, before gripping my hips and pulling me into him with each thrust. "So fucking sexy laid over my bike." He licks his lips. "Look at those tits bounce for me."

"Mmm…," I moan. "Does your bike look better with me on it? With my tits bouncing for you?"

"Everything looks better with you on it. Such pretty boobs my girl has."

"Oh…, Zade."

His thrusts never quicken. He moves with practiced ease and deliberation. I'd wonder how many girls he's fucked on his bike, but I'm far too focused on how good each ridge of his cock feels as he thrusts inside me. He stretches me so good; so perfect.

I tighten my legs around him and let him use me. Submitting to him is the greatest pleasure in the world. He never lets me go unsatisfied while he takes all he needs. I know he's close by how thick his dick is inside me. And just that feeling makes my walls spasm; my thighs tremble. I look at him. He looks like chaos, yet my perfect peace. His eyes are like a remedy to the storm brewing inside me. The one that's about to explode into a screeching whirlwind of true love.

"Fuck…," Zade rumbles. "So fucking tight and wet for me. Come for me, and don't you dare fucking look away." He keeps thrusting into me. One hand moves to my clit and starts rubbing it to the pace of his thrusts. The other moves to my throat.

"Zade!" I scream. Too many sensations are flowing through me, and they all come gushing out of my pussy as my hips jerk into him. I arch off the bike and squeeze my pussy around his dick.

"Blair!" Zade shouts as he releases all of himself into me. We both pant as we spasm and tremble against each other. "Fuck… yes… Squeeze it, baby. Empty it."

My body obeys him without any hesitation. I greedily squeeze every last drop out of him. He slows his rubs on my clit. Once he stops, he helps me up. His dick is still deep inside me, and I don't want to let him go. I love feeling this connection with him.

I jump a little when my phone goes off and sigh. Not wanting to know what Max wants this time, I don't bother reaching for it.

"Is he still texting you?"

"It's non-stop. Even with the new number. I don't know how he got it. I blocked him everywhere."

"Pretty easy to find a number. What about social media?"

I shrug and pull away from him a little. "He just makes new accounts. I have like fifty accounts blocked at this point. He messages me so many different times a day. I don't know. Maybe it's closer to a hundred. I lost track."

His eyes turn to ice as he nods. "It's time I end this."

I narrow my eyes at him. "You mean 'we'."

"I absolutely don't. You're no longer involved from this point forward." He leans in and kisses me as he slowly pulls out of me. I whimper at the loss, and he chuckles as he rights my panties and shorts. "Be my good girl. Go inside. Take a nice, hot bath. Use the jets. I need to go for a couple hours, but I'll be back, and I'll take good care of you, okay? I'll text you so you can order takeout. We can watch a movie if you want. Anything you need."

"Where… are you going to go…?"

He cups my chin. "Nowhere you need to be concerned with." He leans in and kisses me sweetly before gripping my hips and helping me off the bike as he gets off. "Lock the doors, baby. Just go relax. Read a book. Anything you want."

"Okay…?" I bite my lip after he kisses me again. He taps my ass before he packs himself away.

I give him a soft smile as I slowly make my way back to the house thinking about what he's planning. I look over at him once I reach the door. He's backing his bike out, the same bike we just fucked on. I open the door and close it behind me when the garage door closes. I hear the rumble of his bike starting and then taking off.

I don't know what he's about to do, but whatever it is, I trust him with my whole heart and soul. He owns them both anyway.

Chapter Ten

Zade

I've always lived my life with a 'do now, ask forgiveness later' attitude. It's served me well, so far, but tonight… Tonight is one of those nights that makes me question if I'll lose all that's important to me.

Blair.

She's what's important.

My soul was sold long ago, so what I'm about to do won't have any effect on me or my feelings. I know the Reaper's coming for me. It's her I'm worried about.

I drive my bike off my property but slow down and narrow my eyes. I don't live in a very populated area, and I like it that way. What I don't like is seeing a glimpse of a red vehicle on my property that I know isn't mine. Looking closer, I can tell it's Max's.

Good. Saves me from having to track that fucker down.

I shut my bike off and walk it back towards the car. The closer I get, the easier it is to see that he's not around his car.

Which means he's somewhere on my property.

Too close to Blair.

I quickly prop my bike on its kickstand and take out my phone. Probably saw me leaving and decided he was in the clear. I chuckle. Little does he know. I pull up my cameras and see him almost immediately heading to the front door as he checks out my house like he's looking for an entrance point.

"You won't find one, asshole," I mumble. I call up one of my buddies as I stealthily walk towards my house. The guy is dangerous. Very dangerous. Not someone I'd want to mess with.

"Yeah," he answers.

"I need your help, man. Max is around my house."

"You know what to do. Meet you there."

I do know what to do. I hang up the phone and put it back in my pocket. It's dark. Max isn't going to see me coming, and no one is ever going to know he was here once I'm finished with him.

When I found out about Max, I called my friend immediately. He can get things done. I've used him to get rid of problems for me before. Not that I'm afraid to get my hands dirty. I just don't want anything to come back on me. That's what I have him for. It pays to be friends with the leader of a gang.

I sneak up on Max, and before he can turn around, he's in a sleeper hold. I'm a lot bigger than he is. A lot faster. As he drops to his knees, I lean in and whisper in his ear. "I warned you so many times to leave her the fuck alone, man. This is on you."

Without another word, I twist his neck quickly until I hear a satisfying snap. His body instantly goes limp. Wasting no time, I pick him up and put him over my shoulders like I'm carrying him away from a fire.

A fire he fucking started and I ended.

I haul him back to his car and wrestle with his lifeless body as I put him in his trunk. I'm wearing gloves so I have no worries for prints being found, but it's not going to matter anyway. There's a small steel plant not far away from my house that my friend owns and uses for all of his nefarious purposes. To the government, though, it's all on the up and up. His books are meticulous.

I drive Max's car to the plant and let myself in. I drive to the back where the molten steel vats are. My friend is already there leaning against his truck. I get out of the car as he walks towards me.

"Hey, Z. What you got for me?"

"Hey, Xander. Remember that rich dick who keeps getting away with all of these assaults?"

"The one we were talking about after his last hearing ended? Couldn't believe he got off?"

"I haven't had the chance to catch you up, but he went after my girl. Blair. This was before we were really anything more than what I thought we were in my own fucking mind, but I had a tracker on her. Fucking glad I did because…" I trail off and walk him to the truck. I pop it open.

Xander's eyebrows raise as he chuckles. "He went after your girl, so you snapped his neck."

"Damn right. Because after I showed up and took her away, I took her to her house. A couple of hours after we got there, he showed up. Threw some cocktails, and started it on fire. Lit my bike up. Her house. Everything. We went back a couple days later and salvaged her safe, but that's all we could get. He was there that day, too, but I got her away. He's been texting her, calling her, stalking her social media. She blocks him. He creates a new account. Cops won't do anything for her because of who he is."

"Max. Sounds like a pompous name."

"His dad's a big shot attorney. Thinks he can go up against me."

Xander chuckles again. "What do you want done?"

"Well, I killed him. Can't have my hands tied to this. I especially don't want Blair to know. I don't want him to be found."

"Does she know anything about you?"

"She knows what she needs to. She knows I didn't have the best life. I was into a lot of shit when I was younger. She knows I likely still am, but she doesn't say anything. Maybe one day I'll tell her some of the fucked up things I've done, but not now. I'm definitely not telling her that I have a literal body count."

"A fairly significant one, too. What is this? Seven?"

"Lucky number seven. All bad guys. All in self-defense."

Xander grins. "Get home to your girl. I got this douche. I'll take the car, too. Good to chop up." He tosses me his keys to his vehicle. "Park it near your house. I'll grab it later."

I nod. "Thanks, man. And again. I don't want Blair to know any of this. Ever. I don't want this side of my dark touching her light. If she finds out, she'll leave. I'd never allow that. She and I will both die that day."

"Go home, Z. Leave my pay in the visor."

"You mean this pay?" I take an envelope out of my back pocket and hand it to him with a grin.

"Asshole." Xander laughs as he starts taking Max out of the trunk.

"You think I'd ever leave you without pay?"

"Go. I have work to do." Once he has Max out, he takes the envelope from me and shoves it in his back pocket as he turns. I head for his truck and drive home.

The second I'm home and inside, I smell something far too delicious to pass up, but it's Blair dancing around my kitchen that has all parts of me firing at the same time.

She's wearing nothing but an apron as she cooks.

I don't remember the last time someone cooked for me, but it was never this sexy. Her perky little ass is on full display. I take off my gloves and shoes, not wanting to alert her that I'm home. As I walk over to her, she starts singing into a wooden spoon. I start taking off my belt. Her hips sway to the music of *Unforgiven* by Ryan Jesse, and I can't help but think this is the perfect song to be playing right now.

I grip Blair's naked hips and spin her. She squeaks and looks up at me with wide eyes, but I don't give her an option to say anything. I claim her mouth with mine. The feral side of me takes over. All I want is her.

"How much time do I have before whatever smells so good is done cooking?"

Blair glances around me. "It's homemade pizza. You have eleven minutes."

"Perfect." I lift her. She wraps her legs around my waist and her arms over my shoulders. She hangs on well enough for me to push down my jeans before gripping her ass and slamming into her.

I fuck her in the middle of the kitchen. I don't need a wall or counter. All I need is her. We meet each other's thrusts like we're both starved for each other. She's so tight. Fucking warm and wet. She takes me so well.

"Zade!" She digs her nails into my shoulder blades, making me groan.

"Fuck yes, baby."

Her pussy grips me even tighter. I know she's close. I grip her ass and thrust faster, harder, and deeper, pulling her into me until she's screaming for me. Her pussy is so wet, and the sound turns me on even more because I made her like that. I'm the one who turned her into a mess.

And it's all for me.

She's all for me.

She'll never know all I've done for her; all I will do for her, but she'll always know one thing.

She's mine.

The End

Other Books By Melony Ann

The Beautiful Dream Series

Available Now

Loving You
My Love, My Heart
Softening Lyric
Undercover Temptations
Captain Charming
Breaking Boundaries
Crashing Into You
Tactical Inferno
Ravishing Our Queen
Cherished By The Texan
Unveiling Our Passions

Box Sets Available

The Beautiful Dream Series: Box Set: Part 1
The Beautiful Dream Series: Box Set: Part 2

The Crane Family Series

Available Now

The Reluctant Mafia King
Sweet Lies
Billion Dollar Love Story
Be Mine
Protecting Her
Dangerously Forbidden Love
His Heart
Love In The Dark

Box Sets Available

The Crane Family Series

The Deimos Trilogy

Available Now

Connor's Legacy
Aryan's Alpha
Kade's Redemption

Box Sets Available

The Deimos Trilogy

The Forbidden Temptation Series

Available Now

The Detective's Forbidden Temptation
The Running Back's Forbidden Temptation
The Prez's Forbidden Temptation
The Coach's Forbidden Temptation
The Tight End's Forbidden Temptation

The Lucinio Family Series

Available Now

Rising From The Ashes
The Player's Rebel
Encrypting My Heart
Fighting My Fate
Phoenix Rising
Defending Her Honor

Snowed In Trilogy

Available Now

Snowed In For Christmas
Snowed In With The Stalker
Snowed In With My Best Friend

Multi Author Series

Piper Falls: Firehouse 49

Available Now

Ignite My Fire by Melony Ann
Regain My Fire by Kindra White
Playing With My Fire by D.L. Howe
Fight My Fire by Darley Collins
Against My Fire by Anneke Boshoff
Relight My Fire by Louise Murchie
Harness My Fire by Ayana Lisbet
Quench My Fire by Havana Wilder

Piper Falls: Station 28 Series

Available Now

Embracing My Duty by Melony Ann
Torn By My Duty by Kayla Baker
Against My Duty by Anneke Boshoff
Defying My Duty by D.L. Howe
Leave Of My Duty by Nikki A. Lamers
Fulfilling My Duty by Havana Wilder
Following My Duty by Louise Murchie
Replete In My Duty by Stacy Kristen
Accepting My Duty by Darley Collins

Let's Be Friends

Follow me on

Bookbub

Facebook

Goodreads

Instagram

Tik Tok

Visit my website
www.melonyannauthor.com

Subscribe to my newsletter and get a FREE never-seen-before NOVELLA just for subscribers!
https://www.melonyannauthor.com/exclusive-content

Join my Facebook Reader Group!
Melony Ann's Sizzling Book Nook

Acknowledgements

To my loves.

To my friends.

To my team.

To the Bookstagram Community.

To my family.

To all of those who believe in me and support me.

To all of those who don't.

Cover by: Carter Cover Designs

About Melony Ann

Melony Ann began writing short stories and poetry as a child. She continued honing her craft over the years until she took the plunge and began publishing her work, despite having severe anxiety.

Melony is an award winning author, winning a coveted Firebird Award, and writes contemporary romance stories that are full of suspense and a lot of steam.

When she isn't writing, she is loving her family and working to make her life something she deserves.

Melony believes that if her writing can inspire just one person, then all of her hard work is worth it.

Her hope is that her writing allows each and every one of her readers to escape for a little while. To dive into a different world one book at a time.

www.ingramcontent.com/pod-product-compliance
Lightning Source LLC
LaVergne TN
LVHW010943110826
845149LV00013B/2731

* 9 7 8 1 9 6 1 9 6 6 8 1 9 *